O'Brian's

an

Tales From an Irish Pub

By Conley Stone McAnally

PHARAOH PUBLISHING USA

Also by Conley Stone McAnally

Tales From Homer

Tales From the Lake

Wilson Bay: Tales From an Eskimo Village

Jump, Alaska: Tales From the Interior

O'Brian's Black & Tan
Tales From an Irish Pub
By Conley Stone McAnally

Edited by Richard Andrews

PHA013 • ISBN 978-0692364253

Pharaoh Publishing USA
www.pharaohpublishingusa.com

Cover art used under license

Produced and designed by Seann McAnally

For Bev, who said she'd never marry an Irishman.

The Irish

Be they kings or poets or farmers
They're a people of great worth—
They keep company with the angels
And bring a bit of heaven to Earth...
—Anonymous

Contents

A Short Prologue from "Jump, Alaska"

There were only two weeks left in the school year. Our one or two weeks had turned into almost nine months and Bev and I had to make a decision. I had been offered contracts for the upcoming school year from the District and University for more money than I had ever made before in my life, and given the fact that my expenses were very minimal, the amount of discretionary income available staggered a boy from Independence. We had been able to save a lot and it looked like we could save a lot more. A few years like the last one would find us set for life. Money had never been a motivating influence for Bev or me. But then again, given the fact I had nothing better to do, at least at the time I was reading my contract, I had no real reason not to return. We could visit the kids this summer, spend a month or so at our place in Tucson, and return to the wilds and mysteries of Alaska in early September. I was just about ready to sign the contract when there came a knock at the door.

It was Big Bear decked out in his Western Union outfit delivering another telegram. It was from my brother Brian and sister Traci.

"Dear Sir Snapper," the telegram began, "[stop] Sorry we have not kept in touch more frequently [stop] We have exciting news and opportunity but need your help [stop] Don't make any plans for this summer before you talk to me [stop] Will call you this evening with details [stop] Love Brian and Traci [stop]"

Well, Brian was always coming up with some sort of scheme, and my first reaction was to send back a telegram reminding him of the last time he sent such a message. That message ended up costing me a few dollars and a lot of grief.

At one time he wanted to open up a Greek Bar and Grill near his home in Chicago. He was very well connected with the Greek community via his marriage to a nice Greek lady and just knew such a business would be a real money-maker. He had it all planned out. Greek food, Greek music, Greek dancers, Greek décor, and waiters and waitresses that spoke nothing but Greek. He said that the place would even be blessed by the local Greek Orthodox Priest. He just needed a little more start-up money. Our father had died not too long before and left us a little life insurance. He knew I still had money available. I really didn't need the money, so I figured why not.

He did open the place, but then a few things happened that sort of put a crinkle in things. He failed to tell me that he was running a high stakes poker game in the back room that the IRS didn't appreciate, the INS didn't condone the manner in which he conscripted the cooks, waiters and waitresses, and Ouzo became his drink of choice. What little profits there were sort of vanished between the poker games, the anise-flavored beverage, a divorce, and attorneys.

Bev tried to take care of the situation by placing a few strategic, cryptic phone calls to her friends that she thought still remained in Chicago, only to find out that most of them were no longer available, having either left town suddenly, moved to Joliet as guests of the government or, through her contact with the Federal District Attorney's Office, had moved on to places known only to the folks who ran the witness protection program.

Well, needless to say the Greek Bar and Grill went belly-up. The only good thing that happened was that Brian and I had no legal repercussions after all was said and done, and to his credit, after liquidation of all assets, my investment was salvaged and returned.

So I looked upon his telegram with some skepticism to say the least. The only reason I did not immediately send off the contracts for the next school year was the fact that Traci seemed to be involved. She always had a level head and would not be part or parcel to any of Brian's shenanigans. Besides, he was my brother. I would hear him out.

Sure enough, that evening I received a conference call from Brian and Traci. I won't try to transcribe the exact conversation but the gist of the call was this: Brian and Traci were living in Ireland in the

County of O'Malley in a little village called Devere, just a day's train ride from Shannon. Apparently we three had inherited a pub, the only pub in Devere. He and Traci had flown to Ireland to check the inheritance out after Traci had verified that the inheritance was real. The Irish solicitor could not find me, and neither Brian or Traci wished to contact me until they had checked things out, given my foray into that Greek Bar and Grill business. Sure enough, the inheritance was real, the place was quaint, it only needed a little work to get it up to snuff and the best part was that no one wanted me to write a check.

They knew that I would be off during the summer and that Bev had experience running such establishments. They wanted us to come over and help get the place off the ground. Their first two months of operation had been successful and would be even better with our input, but they realized that a third and fourth person were desperately needed to lessen the workload and save their sanity. Would we please come over and help? To top things off, he would buy the airline tickets out of his share of the profits already made.

It did not take me very long to decide what to do, and as I was about to discuss the matter with Bev, I discovered she was already packing.

I only had two question for Brian and Traci: What was the 'Sir Snapper' business, and who the heck would leave us an Irish pub?

I started to check things out just to make doublecertain that Brian was not full of blarney. While Bev busied herself packing for our upcoming trip to the Emerald Isle, I spent my time on the computer.

Charles McAnally came to America after being press-ganged by sailors that were looking for an additional crew member. We know he came from either Belfast or Glasgow or perhaps both. Charles had several sons after he arrived in America, one of which was named Huge. Huge ended up marrying a lady named Elizabeth De'Vere. There was a lot of information about Elizabeth and the De'Vere family.

Her father was the fourth son of Robert De'Vere, the 18th Earl of Oxford, who was sent to Ireland to manage the family holdings because his three older brothers had either inherited the title, gone into the Church of England, or joined the military, and there was nothing left for him to do in England. Apparently Elizabeth's father was not a very good estate manager, for the De'Vere's holdings in Ireland went bankrupt and the De'Veres of Ireland moved to America, leaving Elizabeth's younger brother, Albert, behind in a small house in a much smaller Irish crossroads village. Elizabeth eventually met and married Huge McAnally in America.

Albert was apparently much more adept in business than his father, because he started a little business selling Irish cakes and pies to passersby. This eventually grew into an inn and pub. The locals started calling the place De'Vere's, and the establishment was handed down from one son to another until there were no sons left to run the place, which apparently happened several years ago. The pub had seen better days and remained vacant for a very long time, but the village had been re-named Devere. The Village Council decided to demolish the long-standing pub because it was in ruins anyway, but a member of the Devere Historical Society stepped in and raised such a fuss that the Council relented—but only if the Society could find the rightful owners to restore the place and re-name the pub, because they did not think it proper for a pub to be named after the town. The search began.

While searching though some old records the Society found Albert's will, which stated that if for some reason no son of the De'Vere line was living in Devere, that the establishment should be given to the direct descendants of his beloved sister Elizabeth. That ended up being Brian, Traci and me, as best anyone could tell, and this was certified by the Royal Irish Inheritance Act of 1754. That is how we became owners of the nameless pub in Devere.

The 'Sir Snapper' comment in Brian's telegram was based on the fact that we are descendants of English Royalty, and the Earls of Oxford are part of our bloodline, which can be traced back to 280 AD. That is staggering. I don't know if a 'Sir' is appropriate, given the fact that I have never been knighted even though I am the oldest of the remaining line. I have thought about sending Queen Elizabeth II a note just in case it was overlooked.

Chapter 1
The Trip Over There

Bev had always told me that she never goes anywhere on a plane without something going wrong. I have always thought that to be a wee bit of an exaggeration because nothing of any consequence happened when we flew to Alaska. Well, that is not entirely true. Our plane did abort its takeoff when we left Tucson, and the cabin door got stuck and wouldn't open for an hour when we landed in Anchorage, but things happen. No big deal. However, our trip to Ireland proved to me that perhaps there was something to what she said and caused me to seriously consider booking passage on a steam ship when it came time to return to the States. Unless, of course, the name of the ocean liner was the Titanic II, Lusitania II, the Andrea Doria II, or something like that.

Our flight was to be nonstop to Shannon, Ireland and as soon as we took off, Bev went immediately to sleep. About two hours out of Anchorage, the Captain came over the intercom and asked if there was a doctor or some sort of health practitioner on board. A few minutes later, the Captain came back over the intercom to announce that we would be making an emergency medical landing in Yellow Knife, Canada. Several of the passengers asked our Flight Attendant what the problem was, but she declined to provide us with any information but for us not to worry. "We won't be long in Yellow Knife" is all we could get out of her.

I found out later that a man had been found dead in First Class and the Air Marshall and Captain thought it only prudent to land at the nearest airport and remove the body. The Air Marshall would not have been involved normally but the dead man's sister raised such a fuss that the Marshall had to be called upon to quiet her down. She said her brother was going back to Ireland to die anyway and since he had already purchased a ticket she did not understand what the big deal was. I sort of agreed with her.

The Flight Attendant was correct; we were only in Yellow Knife for a short while. The body was unloaded and we took off without wasting very much time. Bev remained asleep through all of this.

A little while later, the Captain came over the intercom again and said we would have to land in Bangor, Maine to change crews. We found out later that it was because of our stop in Yellow Knife. It was not possible and against regulations to travel across the Atlantic within the time limits established by Ireland's version of the FAA and the Irish Pilots Union, without changing crews. To the credit of Aer Lingus the crew swapped places in record time and off we went. Bev was asleep during all of this.

I finally settled down and tried to sleep, thinking there would be no further problems while crossing the Atlantic. I am not a nervous flier but don't really care for it. I have always maintained that if God wanted man to fly he would have had him be born with a boarding pass. I cannot sleep on an airplane, and thought of waking Bev to see if she wanted to play cards or something, but decided to let her be.

A couple of hours went by when our new Captain came over the intercom and told us that we had to make an emergency landing in Reykjavik, Iceland. This caused a little commotion in the economy class. The commotion was of such a nature that Bev changed positions once in her seat. The Captain did assure us, however, that it was only a safety precaution, that some sort of light had come on and they just wanted to check it out before we finished the last leg of our trip.

We were only on the runway for twenty minutes, so the light must not have been that big of deal, but I did notice that the Co-Pilot got off the plane and met a pizza delivery van and exchanged a handful of money for one large pizza. I do have a suspicious mind and began to wonder about the so-called emergency. But no matter, I concluded after we got underway again. Bev was fast asleep.

A couple more hours passed, and as I was just about to drift off to sleep, the Captain came on the intercom. "Ladies and gentlemen, we have started our descent into Shannon, Ireland, temperature is 12.4 C, wind out of the west south west, overcast with possible rain expected this afternoon. Local time is 9 p.m. Attendants, prepare for landing."

The landing went smooth enough with only one minor bump. As we were taxiing to our gate Bev woke up. She stretched and said "Well, that was a pretty uneventful trip."

Chapter 2
Our Greeting

As we entered the terminal we saw a man holding a sign that read "McAnally." We identified ourselves as being two and he said, "Welcome to Ireland. My name is Connor and I am here to escort you to the next phase of your journey. Please follow me." I asked about our bags and he said his man would pick them up and put them on the train for us. I was a little skeptical about letting all our worldly possessions out of my direct control and trusting them to a stranger, but what were the odds?

We took a short limo ride to the train station and Connor was as good as his word. He escorted us to our compartment and our baggage was already there. He handed us tickets to what I assumed would be Devere, made a slight bow and then just stood there with his hands folded in front of him. Bev nudged me in the side with her elbow and I said, "Oh, yes," and handed him a five dollar bill.

As the train was pulling out of the station the conductor came by, asked for our tickets and told us to enjoy our trip to Beganborn. I told him there must be some mistake. He looked at the tickets again and said, "No, there's no mistake, it clearly says on the ticket here that you are traveling to Beganborn."

"No," I said, "we were supposed to be heading for Devere."

"Well I understand now why the confusion," he replied. "One has to go to Beganborn and catch the cart ride to Devere." There was no problem, he assured us. The carts run every day or two and usually on time.

About two hours later, after a short stop to allow sheep to cross the tracks, the conductor came around again and announced, "Beganborn in five minutes." Bev and I quickly gathered our belongings and got off the train as soon as it stopped.

As the train pulled out, I saw no one around and the little train station was locked up. There was a bench, so we sat on it and waited around for something to happen. Soon a dilapidated cart came lumbering down the cobblestone path that I gathered connected the station to what I assumed would be the center of Beganborn. The cart was pulled by the poorest excuse for a horse I had ever seen. It was lop-eared like a rabbit, had a sway back and was pulling a dilapidated two-wheel cart driven by a man that did not look much better.

"Are you Sir Snapper and Lady Bev?" he asked.

"Yes."

"Toss your things in the cart here, it will only be a short ride. Sir, you ride in back with the luggage, and Lady, you ride up here with me." We then clip-clopped down the road, through the little hamlet of

Beganborn, which seemed like a nice little place. I thought to myself, if Devere looks anything like this, it will be a delightful summer.

However, the further we journeyed from Beganborn, the more bleak the countryside became. The stone walls on either side of the road were crumbling, the road was mud and ruts, the fields were overgrown, what few sheep we saw looked like they had the mange, and the stone houses were deserted and in much need of repair... Brian had done it again, I thought to myself.

The only thing that kept me from dwelling on fratricide was that Traci was part of all this and would not do anything particularly harmful, and besides, I would not know what to do with Brian's body.

As I was about to tell the cart driver to turn around and take us back to the train station, we came over a rise and there in the valley below stretched a lakeside village that was only half as big as Beganborn, but much more typical of what one imagines when one thinks of an Irish Village. I immediately thought of the old musical "Brigadoon," and I started humming the signature tune.

At the top of the hill, the driver turned to us and said, "Welcome to Devere, County of O'Malley, along the Lake Donnie Man." There was a twinkle in his eye and his smile stretched out his wrinkles and made his warts disappear. The horse's ears and back straightened, stone walls and houses were well-maintained, and both nestled up to clean well-kept green fields.

Bev and I proceeded down the path and entered the village of Devere, into what was to be our next great adventure.

Chapter 3
Devere

Brian and Traci were ecstatic to finally meet Bev. The three of them took an immediate liking for one another. After showing us to our room and allowing Bev and me to freshen up a bit, they took us on a tour of the pub and the town.

The pub looked like what you would expect an Irish pub to look like. There was a sign protruding from just over the entrance, but without a crest or a name. Walnut ceiling beams and wall joists were exposed against a white stucco background. There was a dart board in one corner along with a slate blackboard that one could keep score and place P's and Q's as the dart throwers drank their pints and quarts. The tables, chairs, and benches were of dark oak and occupied by characters that must have come out of central casting. The bar was a long dark wooden affair with several draft handles growing though the top, and the wall behind was lined with every sort of alcoholic beverage one could imagine. The schnapps alone were of more flavors than I thought existed.

Devere itself was just as quaint. We were shown

the post office, the Catholic Church—named St. De'Vere of course—the barbershop, meat and fresh produce market, laundry, tailor, bakery, local newspaper, and were introduced to all those who owned and operated them.

At the Town Hall we met the mayor, town council and police chief along with the president of the Devere Historical Society, Mrs. O'Malley. She had been the driving force in restoring the pub and was especially pleased to meet us. Mrs. O'Malley thought that it would be a proper thing for us all to have dinner and a few drinks tomorrow evening to celebrate the arrival of the new co-owners at the pub, and we all readily agreed. Brian was a little hesitant, I could tell, but I did not say anything to him at the time.

On our way back to the pub Brian's mood improved as he waved and spoke to all the lasses that passed. Traci beamed and kept a coy and flirtatious smile on her face as she only nodded to the lads that seemed to cross the street just to tip their hats and wish her a good day. It is the McAnally charm I guess. They take after me. All the men in Devere seemed to be good-looking, the women appeared strong, and I was sure all the kids were above average like in Lake Wobegon. Bev reached out and held my hand, as if establishing property rights, so no Irish wench would think I was available.

As we all four sat in one corner of the pub drinking a black and tan, except for Bev, who does not drink often and only then in much moderation, I asked Brian why he seemed a little hesitant about the dinner tomorrow night. Traci averted her eyes and cast them upon a young man who had just entered and excused herself to speak to him. Brian looked at me, then Bev. She got the hint and excused herself, saying she wanted to check to see what was in the kitchen and how it was arranged.

"That's the problem." And he pointed to Bev walking away.

"I thought you really liked Bev," I said, surprised.

"Oh no," he said, "it's is the kitchen, or what comes out of the kitchen, I should say. It's our cook. He makes the best lamb stew you have ever tasted. The problem is, that's all he knows how to make. The townspeople are getting sick of it and have started to bring in their own sandwiches from the meat market and only buy drinks. Besides, I'm getting pretty sick of it too, and starting to do the same. Doesn't make for a good marketing plan when the owner doesn't eat the food prepared in his own establishment. I told the Town Council and Mrs. O'Malley that my brother, you, and his new wife, were excellent cooks and would be expanding our menu."

"Well," I said, "I don't think that will be a problem, I have a lot of old Irish recipes floating around in my head that were handed down by our grandfather, and Bev is a tremendous cook and can make much out of nothing."

"It is pretty short notice," he said. "You think Bev

is up to it?"

"It isn't a problem, take my word for it," I said emphatically. "Barmaid, bring us another round and leave that poor boy in the corner alone."

Traci brought the drinks right away.

****

After Bev's inspection of the kitchen, Brian told her about his apprehension concerning dinner the next evening. Bev said she thought the kitchen was clean and in good order and the cook, Abdul, was a very pleasant fellow and was not threatened at all that she would apparently be taking over the Executive Chef position. In fact, he welcomed the change. He too had become weary of his lamb stew.

Bev brought out a tablet and pencil, made some notes and gathered us around a table over black and tans. "Here is what we need to do today so we are on top of things tomorrow evening. Brian, you go across the lake to Rockenshire and pick up a barrel of Chianti. Tell Jarome we want the good stuff he keeps behind the boat dock." I looked at her in a puzzled way. She had only been here less than three hours. How did she know about Rockenshire, and who the heck was Jarome? I was about to ask but she anticipated my question. "Jarome's great uncle and my great uncle used to do business together. Great Uncle Solito used to import wine and Irish Whiskey from him back in the late 20's."

"The late 1920's? Why that was during pro… Oh."

and I dropped the subject.

"Traci and I will go to the meat and fresh produce market and pick up a few things. Abdul, you stay here and mind the store and watch the P's and Q's, especially your own."

"What about me?" I inquired.

"As far as I can tell, you have not slept for over 24 hours. Go to bed," she said with authority. She was in her element, I could tell.

****

When I woke the next morning, I noticed the smell of Italian red sauce. Bev had pulled it off and I was not surprised.

That evening, the meal was a hit. Spaghetti, meatballs, Italian sausage, baguettes, olive oil laced with Romano Cheese and garlic were devoured by all present. If it had not been impolite to clamor for more the throng would have. Mrs. O'Malley and the mayor told us that they were very impressed and knew that the pub would once again become the social center of the village and county.

I knew we all loved spaghetti and meatballs but also knew that we could not serve such a dish all the time or folks would be looking upon the Italian feast like the lamb stew before long. I broached the subject Monday morning over biscuits and tea.

Bev said her plan was simple. As far as Abdul, he was very capable of learning how to prepare different kinds of food, but he needed to focus on one thing at a time. Also if we had a full menu slate like most restaurants, the spoilage would be greater, causing waste thus depleting profits. Her solution was to have a specialty each day. That way Abdul could keep focused on what he did and we could buy specific items for specific days and if planned correctly, what was left over could be used for the next meal the next day or maybe even the day after that. She also said that we all had to specialize in a specific area, but cross-train as much as possible so we all could get a day off now and then and fill in when one of us fell ill.

The daily meals would consist of pasta on Sunday, chicken noodle soup on Monday, potato soup on Tuesday, Polish sausage and sauerkraut on Wednesday, tacos and barbeque on alternating Thursdays, catch of the day from the boats in the harbor on Friday, and baked chicken and boiled potatoes on Saturday. On holidays we would serve lamb stew, and she was sure that the villagers would flock to eat it because it was not the quality but the frequency everyone complained about. We would not serve breakfast, but always have plenty of biscuits available for the early morning crowd. As far as lunch went, she would arrange for the meat market and bakery to provide a tray of meat and bread each day on a consignment basis, and we would take a 10% handling charge based on the sandwiches sold.

As far as our responsibilities went, Brian would procure all the liquor and food needed for the following week and stage it in the kitchen. He would also be the chief bartender.

Abdul would keep the kitchen clean, wash dishes, and assist in food preparation, sort of like a sous-chef. Abdul loved what he saw as a new title.

Traci would wait tables and tend bar. Bev said Traci would be the heart of the operation and key to its success. Bev had observed that Traci turned the eye of every young man in Devere, and given a little more cleavage on Traci's part, more men would flock to the pub. The more men that came to the pub the more the young girls would come, and the more young girls, the more old men, and the more old men, the more old women.

Bev said she would supervise Abdul, keep the books, plan special occasions, and be in charge of entertainment.

Well, I was beginning to feel like the redheaded stepchild. What was to be my job, I wanted to know. Bev said, "Back-up for everyone else and our ambassador of good will. You will regale the patrons with stories of your travels and engage them in intellectual conversation. In other words, sit around and lie to them as they lie to you to see who can tell the bigger lie. Believe me, next to Traci it is the most important job here."

There was only one more thing to decide. Mrs. O'Malley had insisted that we not call the pub Devere. Her reasoning was never quite clear but had something to do with Devere not being associated with drunks and hooligans like so many Irish villages were. “We don’t mind a pub in our village of course, in fact we need one, but we do not have to let the whole world know that we consider a village and a pub one in the same.”

We tossed around several names like just plain old Pub or other such nondescript identities like Ye Olde Irish Pub, Irish Pub, McAnally’s, The County Inn, Do-Drop-Inn, Calico Inn, and more. It wore us out. Nothing seemed to click. I put my head down on the table and said, “Oh, Brian, another black and tan, if you please.”

Chapter 4
Killer Sheep

Traci said she would do anything she could to insure that O'Brian's Black &Tan was a success. She had noticed over the last several weeks that there was a lull in business before noon each Saturday, and thought that if some method could be devised to get patrons in earlier, sales would increase in the early morning hours and by virtue of already being there, those present would stay for lunch. Her plan worked.

Every Saturday morning beginning precisely at 9:00 she would take a bucket of soapy water and sponge and begin washing the outside of the windows. Now washing windows in and of themselves would not normally draw a crowd, but she had devised a method of washing four panes at the same time. I will let your imagination conjure up how this task was performed.

There were no seats available near the windows on this one particular Saturday morning, so when O'Gradey came in like he always did around 10:30, he sat at the bar and listened to me finish up a story about the time I tracked a polar bear while living in

Alaska. All were very much impressed.

"So you see my friends, there is not a meaner or more dangerous animal in all the world." I concluded.

O'Gradey, while hunched over his first pint of the day, said that sure enough a polar bear was an animal that deserved respect, but he took issue as to it being the most dangerous animal in the world. "It's undoubtedly the meanest animal in the arctic, but not the world. That would be our killer sheep found not far from here in the Thickets and Hills of O'Clare." The crowd nodded their heads in agreement.

I could not let the comment go unchallenged. "Why, I've never heard of a killer sheep."

"Well, it is nothing we talk about much, it's bad for tourism. In fact I am one of the few men alive that has ever hunted the beast and lived to tell the tale."

This I had to hear. "And what, pray tell, would that tale be?"

That was all O'Gradey needed.

"It was a blustery cold day," he began as the crowd gathered around, except for the young men sitting by the windows pretending not to watch Traci, "and the townspeople of Devere realized that something had to be done. One of the killer sheep had wandered down from the mountains and had been killing pigs, chickens, and peaceful sheep. The Town Council knew that I was a veteran of the troubled times and had spent time traveling the world, having found it only prudent at the time, at least until things cooled down. While in Africa I took up big game hunting and became very proficient in doing so. When I returned to Devere the people knew of my talent and expertise and approached me to track down and destroy the killer sheep that had been harassing them lately, or at the very least chase it back to the Thickets and Hills of O'Clare and do something to insure it would never return. I deemed it my duty to protect our town. Pigs, chickens, peaceful sheep today and our little children tomorrow? Yes, I would take the challenge.

"I went to the place where the last kill was reported. Near the carcass of a bonnie-looking sheep I saw tracks leading back toward the Thickets and Hills of O'Clare. I could tell by the size of the hoofprints and the stride that this was a big one, and that my task was most certainly to be a challenge. I was not deterred, however. I had my spear I had taken off a Zulu warrior and my trusty British Enfield acquired during the troubled times slung over my shoulder.

"I came to the first row of thickets and pressed through, cutting my skin and tearing my clothes but on I went. I proceeded for an hour or so until I stepped in a bog and sunk to my hips. I struggled out of the muck but in so doing I dropped my Enfield and it was sucked down in the mud and disappeared. There was no way of retrieving it. I still had my Zulu spear, so I continued the hunt.

"I clawed and crawled through the thickets that ran uphill for another hour or so. I finally came to a clearing and paused to rest. I must have dozed off, for I was awakened by a sound that immediately put a shiver down my spine. I looked around to where the sound was coming from and saw the biggest killer sheep I had ever seen. Bigger than the one they used to keep stuffed at the terminal at the Shannon Airport until the tourism commission protested. For some reason, though, the killer sheep was not aware of my presence. I silently said a Hail Mary and an Our Father.

"Gently and quietly, I rose to my feet to get in a better position to fling my spear with all my might. The spear found its target just above the sheep's shoulder blade. To my horror, the spear bounced off. The killer sheep turned and set its eyes on me. It snorted like a wild hog, pawed its front hoofs like a raging bull, and charged at me like a white rhino, all of which I had seen before, but never without a weapon in my hand.

"A killer sheep's speed is legendary, but this one seemed faster than legends. The closer he got, the faster he got, and when there was just a few yards separating us, he opened his mouth wide as if to engulf me like the whale did Jonah.

"I stood my ground, knowing I could not outrun the beast, and just as he was about to make me no more I reached inside its mouth with my right arm, plunged it to the rear of the beast, grabbed its stubby tail, pulled back as hard as I could, and turned the creature inside-out. He started running the other way. He is still running as far as I know."

I told Brian to get Mr. O'Gradey a quart of whatever it was he was drinking. On this day, I had been outdone.

Chapter 5
Mic and Mac

McShane and MacDougan were about as much a fixture at O'Brian's Black & Tan as anything else. They would arrive every morning after Mass, sit at the same table in the corner lit only by the Irish morning sun, order a cup of coffee, two shots of whiskey each, then play dominoes till around noon when they went home and took a nap. They would return around 7: 00 p.m. and repeat the process, except they drank Guinness with their shots of whiskey till closing time. During their vicious domino games, sips of coffee, shots of whiskey and glasses of Guinness they would argue. Their sometimes heated banter had no particular topic. If McShane was for it MacDougan was against it. The village had been watching the two battling over the years with great amusement, but never took sides as to who was right and who was wrong.

Their arguments while seemingly very serious, did not deter their friendship. But to the casual observer it was well hidden. Their true feelings had been cemented many years ago by a common tragedy. They were widowers—their wife had died. I say wife and not wives because they had been married to the same woman. When Mary divorced McShane she had married MacDougan and when she divorced MacDougan she left town and married a dairyman from Sallyport a few miles down the road. She was glad to get rid of McShane and MacDougan and looked forward to a life of luxury, for the dairyman was very successful and did not drink. She did not count on the lead milk-cow getting her udder in a ringer and kicking her, Mary, in the head, which I guess one never does count on.

At the funeral McShane and MacDougan started arguing about who was really the widower, giving no credence to the dairyman's claim. The dairyman returned to Sallyport, never to be heard from again in Devere. That was twenty years ago and the two old combatants had argued ever since.

One morning, during an especially heated game of dominoes, MacDougan said that all St. Patrick's Days ought to be celebrated on a Saturday like Easter was on Sunday. McShane said that would be ridiculous. The argument was on.

"How would we know what the proper Saturday would be, if that were the case?" said McShane.

"The same way we know when Easter is, you stupid Irishman." MacDougan responded.

"Well, how do we know that?" snapped McShane.

"It's always on the calendar. You could just look at the calendar...if you knew how to read, you drunken sod," replied MacDougan.

The argument and insults kept going on for about

a half hour when I decided to step in and put in my two farthings worth. It wasn't the brightest thing I ever did.

"All right my fine Irish gentleman," I interrupted, "I do not wish to take a particular side at this point but I think I need to add some reasoning to this banter. If you want to debate you must define your terms and establish some agreed upon facts. First of all, Easter is always the first Sunday after the first full moon after the vernal equinox and St. Patrick's Day is always on the 17th of March. Can we agree on that?" There was a little grumbling and finally they both agreed that the 17th of March was correct but they were not sure if Easter was really established the way I said.

"I know it may be a little confusing," I continued in my professorial tone. "If we want to stay consistent about such things we could stay with the St. Patrick's Day date and change the Easter celebration to a specific day also. The only problem I see with that is that Easter would be celebrated on any day of the week and not just Sunday. If we kept Easter following the vernal equinox tradition, and wanted to keep consistent we could make St. Patrick's Day be the 1st Saturday after Groundhog's Day, or something like that. No, gentleman I think you have been arguing about a system that has lasted for years and done us all very well. McShane, I agree with you. MacDougan, you are wrong."

A hush fell over the Pub. No one had ever taken sides with McShane or MacDougan, at least publicly, in one of their arguments. All were waiting to see what would happen next, while silently agreeing with either McShane or MacDougan.

"Sir," McShane said in an angry voice, "you have just insulted my friend."

"I agreed with you, McShane," I said, perplexed.

"MacDougan may be an ignorant drunken Irish sod, but he is my ignorant drunken Irish sod and not to be insulted by the likes of you," he challenged while raising his shillelagh.

The next morning the local newspaper, reporting the events that followed, used as its lead for the story: "Among the injured were..."

Chapter 6
Snake Eyes

Some people will do or say anything for a free drink.

Traci was washing the windows and drawing her own crowd, Brian was pouring drinks, taking inventory, and flirting with one of the town lassies, Abdul was out back making some foundation repairs, and Bev was cooking up some homemade gravy in the kitchen. I was doing what I do best.

"So you see my fine lads, Alaska was visited by St. Patrick, and just like Ireland, he drove the snakes out. How else can you explain that neither have any?" With that I slammed back the rest of my black and tan, feeling quite the expert and smug about matters that my newfound neighbors and pub-goers knew nothing about. I was fulfilling my duties as host and story teller for our pub while providing a little educational enrichment.

Through the bottom of my glass I could see Mack O'Willy finish off his pint with a slight smirk about his face. He had just returned from Dublin, where he worked in a traveling carnival. The carnival had just played our town and O'Willy decided he was tired of all that stuff and figured he would stay home for awhile. He had just quit and was grimy from head to toe like he had been crawling through the dirt. Typical Carnie attire, I thought to myself, having had Carnies as relatives of my own.

I was unable to attend the two-day carnival affair and didn't want to anyway, because in my youth, I once worked for my cousin providing chickens for the geek he had employed (which happened to be another cousin). I spent more time than one should in such places and all it did for me was to make me detest chicken prepared in any fashion. I worked the bar while Traci, Brian, and Bev sold food at one of the concessions. Abdul puttered around outside between preparing the evening meal and washing dishes.

"You don't believe me, O'Willy,?" I asked

"Oh, I believe it all right, or I should say I believe you believe it, but you are way off about your facts," O'Willy informed. "Most people believe the way you do, but the facts, or I should say some of the facts, like St. Patrick and the snakes, are not true at all, for the most part. I cannot say about Alaska having no snakes or even about our blessed saint actually making it that far west, or possibly north and then dipping south, or going east if he had a mind to. All I know for sure is that there is at least one snake living in our beloved homeland, and it's underneath the floor in the pipe-crawl where we sit."

A hush fell over my patrons and we all seemed to dip our heads and stare at the wooden floor. Then simultaneously we fixed our eyes on O'Willy.

I soon gathered my thoughts and told O'Willy that if he was so sure to put his money where his big mouth was, and bet me a round on the house that he was right and I was wrong. He agreed but said he needed to tell us all a story first. The Irish are always telling a story or two to get across a point that no one else seems to understand.

"You see, pub-keeper and honored patrons," O'Willy began, "we don't have a lot of snakes in Ireland but the ones we do have live a long, long time. When I was just a lad my Grandfather, God rest him, woke me one night and asked me to help get rid of a snake he had seen crawling into a hole under this very pub. Well, Baba, as I called him, had seen a lot of spiders and snakes in his day due to his love of the grain, so it wasn't unreasonable that he woke me at such an early hour, for he had given up long ago trying to get anyone else's attention. How can you turn your sainted grandpa down? Besides, I always liked these midnight adventures of ours. You see, this was not the first time I was awoken to go on a hunt for some sort of creepy-crawly or just to make sure none were keeping his skin company. We never caught a snake however. In fact I never really saw one or any other wiggly reptile or crawling arachnid on or off his body. But I came to realize then as now, it ain't the trophy but the race.

"We made our way to the back of this pub, Devere's as it was called then, where Baba had seen the snake vanish into a hole. Since I was the smaller of the two, naturally, he had me bend down to see if I could see anything in the hole. Well, it being night, all I could see was a bunch of blackness looking back at me, if in fact blackness can look at all. I mentioned such to Baba and he immediately recognized the problem so he took a cigar out of his breast pocket, lit it and puffed to get a red glow. While he was doing that I busied myself digging out around the hole to get a better view to enable me to extend my head and hand under the pub.

"When he figured he had illuminated the end of the cigar enough he handed it to me and I stuck it inside the hole along with part of my head and scanned the area. At first I could see nothing, but then in a distance I saw two little red specks moving from side to side in tandem. It startled me and I, yes I must admit, was scared more than just a little.

"I jerked my head and arm back out of the hole and told Baba what I had seen.

"'Quick lad, let's cover up the hole and trap the monster under the pub. That way he can't get out and will starve to death.

"'But Baba, won't he just find another way out or make a new hole?'

'Heavens no. The Devers have always believed in keeping their family foundation tight and solid and I am sure that applies to their home and pub also. Besides a snake has no arms and he can't dig his way out. The animal will starve to death in no time at all.' But I was not so sure. There were enough mice and soggy ground to keep anything alive and well-fed and watered for many years, and if I were a betting man—and it appears I am—I'm sure the snake is there to this very day. Some reptiles live to be over a hundred years old, you know." O'Willy ordered another pint drained half of it and slammed the glass back on the bar.

As O'Willy finished his story I realized I had him in a trap. Everyone in the pub was going to have a free drink and I was going to make a few more Irish dollars. How could he think that he would be able to outwit me in the art of story telling?

"Alright Mr. O'Willy, even if I were to believe your story, you still have no proof that snakes in general and that particular snake has lived all these many years. How would you know? You never looked back into the hole, did you? How could you, you covered it up. And no foundation is so strong that there won't be a crack or two during the years for a snake to slither through. Just ask Abdul, he has been out all day, like most days doing preventive maintenance on the rock foundation and patching up a recently noticed hole. Ah, a nice story but a story no less, no facts to back it up." I waited for the laughter to die down and ordered a round for the house and waited for O'Willy to pay up.

"Pub-keeper," O'Willy responded, "There is a way to prove my facts. Facts are stubborn, you know. Let's pull up a couple of these planks that make up your floor and you crawl down there with a flashlight and see for yourself. There should be no fear on your part, for two reasons: There are no snakes in Ireland, you say, and secondly, if there was one, it has already left or even died and in no way could hurt you, or scare you—if you are prone to be scared, that is, of a small little slithering reptile."

Ha, I thought to myself. Me afraid of a snake? Never. However crawling around a space small as the crawlspace was a different matter all together. "I tell you what, O'Willy, I am not going to crawl under the pub, but I will stick my head between the two planks we remove and do a visual search with my flashlight." That seemed to satisfy O'Willy.

We cleared away some tables and chairs from the center of the floor while Mic, Mac, O'Gradey and a couple of other regulars began the process of removing the wooden floor planks so I could get my head and shoulders under the floor. As Mic and Mac held my legs, I dipped my body into the hole up to my hips, began my visual search, and as I had suspected, there was no sign of a snake. I yelled back up to the crowd, which was growing, and was about to tell them to pull me out when I heard a noise I could not identify. It was sort of like a springing or hissing sound. I turned the flashlight in the direction of the noise, and there looking at me were two beady eyes, red, moving back and forth in tandem. I yelled for the men to hurry and get me out of there. It seemed like it took longer than it should have, but eventually I was sitting on the floor next to the hole panting and sweating. One of the boys gave me a drink that Brian had waiting and I told the men, "Quick, put the floor back. We'll keep the little devil there for a few more years. Someone tell Abdul to hurry up and finish filling up the holes around the foundation, now! All right, O'Willy you won. Brian, put the drinks on my tab instead of O'Willy's. In fact make it another round." A cheer came from the crowd. I am a poor winner but a gracious loser.

About that time Bev came out of the kitchen followed by Abdul. "What in the name of the Sicilian Gods is going on out here?" I briefly told her sort of sheepishly. She just stood there for awhile then bowed and shook her head. "Look out the window, pub-keeper."

I could see the carnival going past and the last wagon to go by had painted on its side a picture of a snake with two reddish eyes configured in such a way that its eyes seemed to move from side to side in tandem. "Reptilian bobble-heads for sale" was painted in bright red letters under the picture, just above the wheel wells.

Chapter 7
Ray

I have always wondered about homing or migratory instincts. None of our leading scientists that study such things have ever come up with an answer that will pass the rigor of scientific analysis. They seem to content themselves with the description of what and where animals go, but never how they manage to pull it off.

From time to time, I think that perhaps they are making more out of it than they should. I mean, take geese for instance. They leave their happy homes in the far north at a time when they think their water habitat will freeze over and always go to the same place where the water does not freeze, or if it does, not all of it, and if they are real lucky they get fed by a populace that think having geese poop on their lawns and lakebank is adorable. Biologists have wondered for years how they get back to the same location year after year, but to me it doesn't seem that complex. It's like they would just recognize the geography of the earth after a few years of following the leader and memorize the path so when it was their time to be leader they would not get lost. The same could be said about whales traveling from Alaska to Hawaii; they just follow the floor of the ocean. Well, I guess it could be, if whales could see that far through the ocean deep.

However none of this explains how a bird can fly to Hawaii from Alaska with nothing but ocean below their flight path, or how a dog left by its owners in Omaha can find their old masters in Tucson, or even still how Ray the Raven ended up perched on one of the exposed beams of O'Brian's Black and Tan.

Now you might remember Ray the Raven. If not let me jog your memory. When Bev and I lived in our log cabin in what really was an enchanted forest of the Alaskan wilderness, a stranger stopped by one evening. He, as all strangers stopping by, was invited into the house for a warming fire and some tea and biscuits. He had as a traveling companion a raven, which perched on his shoulder as he talked to us (the man, not the raven). The man was a little strange and rambling but every time I asked him about the raven sitting on his shoulder he would ignore me. I would not let the matter drop and eventually the man became very uncivil. He stormed out of the house in a huff because I would not let the matter drop, vowing he would return "nevermore." The Raven stayed, however. I guess it was because he was tired of the man's ravings and being ignored, or perhaps it was Bev's homemade biscuits. Regardless, the Raven and I became very close and he would accompany me on most of my trips to see students scattered around the area. I called him Ray.

The day Bev and I left for Ireland, I told Ray he would have to move on and join his own kind. Ravens don't cry, of course, and I was not sure what Ray really thought about departing, but he took what I thought was a deep breath, turned his head stoically towards the east, flapped his wings for a takeoff, and ventured forth to find his way in the world while we left for Ireland and our next great adventure.

I was awakened one Saturday morning by the crashing and banging of pots and pans coming from the pub kitchen just below our bedroom. By the time I ran out the door to the landing overlooking the bar and dining area, I saw Abdul running around with a fishing net raised over his head. He tripped over tables and chairs and shouted out words which I assumed were in Arabic, for I didn't understand any of what he was saying. He noticed me behind the upstairs railing and pointed to a beam just above my head and to the right. He managed to gasp out the word, "Thanksgiving."

I looked in the direction he was pointing and realized the object of his chase was a huge black bird. To my astonishment, I realized it was Ray the Raven, my friend and companion I had left behind, or at least set free to make his way in the world, when I left Alaska. Ray did make his way in the world, and made it over here.

Ray jumped off his perch and onto my shoulder.

We did not kiss or hug or anything like that, but he nuzzled his beak in my hair with what can only be described as affection.

Bev came out of the bedroom and Ray immediately recognized her, as she did him, and he jumped on her shoulder and started nuzzling her head also. Bev is a soft touch and immediately did what she had to do and left us to accomplish her task.

Abdul was a little taken aback about all this. I quieted him down and the three of us, Abdul, Ray, and I, sat down at one of the tables, where I told Abdul about Ray and how we became friends. Abdul said that he had never seen a raven nor a turkey but had heard us talk about them and couldn't remember which one was eaten during the American Thanksgiving. He knew we had talked about importing a "bird" to celebrate Ireland's Thanksgiving next week and thought the bird had arrived yesterday on his day off and escaped from its cage. He was just trying to catch it with the fishing net.

"Well." I said, "All's well that ends well, it is said." At about this time Bev came from the kitchen carrying some tea and a plate heaped with biscuits.

Chapter 8
What's Up, Doc

Brian was in the back counting money from the local poker game that no one was supposed to know about. Bev was in the kitchen experimenting with a biscuit recipe, watched over very carefully by Ray the Raven. Abdul had gone to Saturday night mass, which I thought strange because he always wanted the Friday Muslim service off, along with any Christian or Jewish holidays that might come along. He claims he just wants to pay homage to all. My guess is that he is hedging his bets. Traci was in the corner whispering in the ear of some young hardbody, and I was once again regaling my customers with the wit and wisdom of which I was and still am so blessed.

"So you see, me fine lads, America has the best medical system and doctors in the world!" And with the word 'world' I slammed my glass tankard of ale down on the bar. Apparently I slammed it a little too hard because it shattered on the hard oak bar top. My hand slipped from the handle, slashing the outside of my palm against the glass shards. A fountain of blood started spewing forth like a Texas oil well, if in fact they still let oil wells spew.

Everyone in the bar was stunned at first, and I was in shock, I guess, because I felt no pain and was mesmerized by the blood gushing out from the side of my hand. MacDougal happened to be sitting beside me and immediately grabbed my wrist to stop the flow of blood. McDaniel, sitting on the other side, grabbed the bar rag and pressed it against my opened wound. Between the hand tourniquet and direct pressure the flow of blood slowed and then stopped altogether.

We all sat there for what in retrospect seemed like a long time, when someone said we ought to get the doctor. Someone else said that somebody would have to go get him, because his car had broken down and he hadn't the money to pay for it until his medical subsidy came in next week. I told them it was not necessary because if we applied enough pressure long enough, coagulation would set in and all would be fine. I remembered that from my Army or Boy Scout days. I couldn't recall which exactly, not that there was that much difference in the training or application of the career. I guess the Boy Scouts did have adult leadership, though.

To pass the time I called for Brian to set up a round for the house. MacDougal and McDaniel started to sweat a little, and I think I even saw a tear come to the eye of McDaniel. "What's wrong with you two? I asked. "I'm the one in harm's way here."

"Yes, we know that," said MacDougal, "It is only that it takes both our hands to keep the blood from spewing out so you won't bleed to death and we are just contemplating how we are going to drink our free pints. Opportunities like this don't come around a lot, you know."

It would have been an easy fix for my sniveling two sods if we had straws available, but we did not serve enough soft drinks to justify the expense. Traci suggested that she could lift the glass up to their lips but McDaniel had a harelip, and the ingredients would fall on his chin, thus wasting the brew and creating bitterness and jealously towards MacDougal and everyone else in the pub, I suspected, because no one else had such a deformity that would cause the spillage.

I must admit that I became very proud of MacDougal and McDaniel when they decided that they could do without for awhile. They thought that coagulation would soon occur and they were determined to put aside their concerns for the good of the community and my hand. They both said they were of sturdy stock. They hunkered down for the duration but their commitment seemed to grow weaker by the minute. They sort of started crumbling before my eyes. You would think they were losing blood. Depression can do strange things to a person, I guess.

After a few minutes we all decided that perhaps the blood had coagulated enough and my two medics slowly released the pressure from my wrist and wound, but as soon as they did the fountain of blood returned and spurt out like the water from

Moby Dick's blowhole. My two medics resumed their positions to stop the flow, more depressed as they realized it would be longer till they got some brew.

"O.K., enough is enough," came a voice from the kitchen door. Bev had been watching all this nonsense for a while and decided that I was not going to bleed to death on her watch.

She instructed one of the boys to fetch Doc Mike and tossed him the keys to the Moped. She too knew that the Doc's car was out of commission and we would all just have to endure the extra time it took to get him and drive him back. Another lad she told to fetch the water hose out back. When the water hose arrived she told Brian to depressurize a keg of beer and stick one end of the hose in it. She then took the other end of the hose and slit it down the middle to a point where eventually she had two half hose-bits. She then took some duct tape and cardboard and made two straw-type looking affairs. "There now, you two stop your whimpering and suck on these while we wait for the Doc." The procedure immediately revived my two saviors and fortified their resolve

Doc Mike showed up later than he would have liked, of course, and immediately went to work. I knew he thought it was somewhat serious because he did not order his usual Merlot prior to his stitching my hand. I must say for an Irishman without the proper American medical training, he did a pretty good job.

I asked him if being without his car caused him problems. He said just a little, but not enough to forgo the extra expense. "I really can't afford two BMWs. I am not an American doctor, you know."

Chapter 9
A Lot of Bull

He pranced around the arena in triumph with his head held high in a majestic pose that called out to everyone that he was superior, he was dominant, he was courageous. He was as bold as he was black.

When I was a young man, I was not what you would call a good athlete, but I was able to rise to the pinnacle of a mediocre career in one sport because, as my football coach said, "You don't mind getting knocked down." The ability to get up from a pounding can serve a person well through the journey of life, but one cannot play body-punishing games after a certain age without future consequences. Ask any NFL player.

Now, my brother Brian participated in the type of games that he could play into adulthood. If you were choosing up sides for almost any adult team event, he would be one of the first ones picked. But regardless, there comes a time when one has to hang up the jock and leave real competition to the young and think in terms of coaching or managing or just watching. Therein lay the crux and subject of this muse.

Brian and I were closing down the pub one evening and he looked a little forlorn. I asked him what the problem was, and he said it was getting close to October and it had just occurred to him that this past summer was the first summer in a very long time that he had not played baseball and that he couldn't play basketball this winter, due to there being no basketball court in Dever. In fact, he said that other than an occasional dart game, there was absolutely no competitive or even non-competitive games taking place anywhere in the village.

I could tell he was still pondering the situation while we kept cleaning and when we were through for the evening I decided we ought to dirty two glasses. Over a black and tan or two I thought I would try to lift his spirits. It was my duty as an older brother to give guidance and solace and care to my younger and weaker siblings. (Which also brought to mind that I was going to have to have a talk with Traci—she was staying out way too late these days—but to continue about cheering up Brian.) I suggested that perhaps we could sponsor some sort of athletic event. He thought that over for a moment and then said that was an excellent idea. (Most of my ideas are excellent and I am sure I stand in front of my kin and peers while they look at me in awe.) So we started our planning process, which consisted first of drawing another black and tan. Now what kind of sporting event should it be?

Football and basketball came to mind, but neither of us could name an Irish football or basketball player. It must not be in the blood (most of the Fighting Irish of Notre Dame are really Polish, and the Boston Celtics are Italian, I have heard.) Besides, outfitting a team and preparing a suitable playing area would be very expensive. Baseball was out because it reminded the Irish of cricket, thus reminding them of the hated English. Golf took too much room; boxing was not seriously considered due to the fact that there were enough fights on Friday and Saturday here at the pub and at every wake and funeral around the community; and soccer and rugby were dismissed because we figured no one wanted to work that hard, at least here in Devere. Boat racing was a possibility because of the lake nearby but the boats at the wharf were more for commercial fishing and cargo, not for sporting. Swimming? Too cold most of the year. Volleyball? Too many short people due to intermarrying with the leprechaun county to the north. Along those lines, we both agreed that Dwarf tossing was a little insensitive and might alienate some of our customers. Horse racing might have been a possibility but those who owned horses used them to pull carts and plows. We thought we came up with a winner when chariot or plow racing sprang to mind, but the carts were old and rickety and I am not sure plow racing is even a sport. If Bev, Abdul, or Traci were at our meeting, bocce ball, camel racing, and spin the bottle would have been suggested, but they weren't, so they weren't. Like Brian said, "Who can get excited over someone throwing big balls at a little one, and most of the town wouldn't be able to climb on a camel because the people are too short and the camels too tall, and Traci would cheat."

Brian eventually grew tired and said, "You know this is all just a bunch of bull, I am tired of wrestling with the problem."

'Epiphany!' or would 'Eureka!' fit better?

****

It was billed as the Devere Bull Wrestling Championship. The village butcher donated an old bull just long enough for us to use it in the championship before it went under the knife. It had just arrived by cart transport, which as I found out later, was the standard mode of transporting a bull in rural Ireland whether it for butchering or breeding.

The bull appeared rather docile and walked around the pen like a whipped pup. He really could be lead by the nose. I think he must have been depressed because he realized that when there were no cows waiting for him in the corral the end was near. The fight had gone out of him.

The object of bull wrestling, Brian and I decided, would be sort of like regular wrestling. The bull would be thrown on its back and made to stay there for 10 seconds one way or another. Now we realized that no one man could take down a bull by himself, so keeping in the spirit of having as many as we could participate, we decided that there should be teams of a 5:1 ratio—that is, five humans to one bull. There was no particular reason for the number five. It was selected because we had five fingers on one hand. Given that reasoning, I guess it could have been 10, 15, 20 or in some cases 21 to one if all digits were counted and a male was doing the counting, but 5 sounded about right.

Seven teams entered in all. All were sponsored by local entities. The Catholic Church had a team of young seminarians who "just happened" to be transferred to Devere prior to the event thus making them eligible. The police department fielded a team, even though they had to use two who were serving a 30-day sentence for nonsupport. There were three family teams whose sons were very large. Being an election year, the mayor sponsored a team that consisted of two women, and even though he was applauded for his diversity it was thought he had very little chance. And of course there was a team representing our pub.

Among the odds-makers it was wagered that O'Brian's Black and Tan would finish next to last behind the Mayor's team. They were probably right at the time because none of my regulars were in any shape to manhandle a bull, and those who were, were already on one of the other teams. Brian and I were not eligible because we sponsored the event, Abdul was not a citizen, he claimed, and Bev and Traci just right-out refused. Through guile and coercion and free drinks for a month we did manage to drum up four sods but were stymied on who would be the fifth.

We were having a training and strategy session around the pub one morning, when a stranger walked in and ordered a pint. He sat at the end of the bar and listened to our 'going nowhere' banter, which mostly consisted of trying to figure out who would be the fifth man on the team.

"Excuse me, gents," the stranger interrupted, "but I seem to understand that you are looking for one more team member. I might be able to help, given some sort of consideration. I just arrived in town and know a little about bulls. You see, I am a Bull Whisperer. The name is Brendan."

****

Our team, led by its captain, Brendan, having been duly elected by the team members with a little help of a pint of two provided by the sponsor, was the last team to try their luck. All other teams had failed. No team even came close. What appeared to be a docile creature when he arrived in Devere had regained some energy when a shipment of cows were herded into the corral next to his. It sort of gave him some vim and vigor and like all lecherous old men, he thought he might have one more time in him. He needed to show off to his new neighbors, is what I guess. Typical male, but we Alpha males have no choice, it is part of our DNA.

I really didn't think our team had any chance at

all, given the plan Brendan laid out, but what did I know. As the bull was prancing about flaunting his stuff and feeling sort of cocky because he had chased all the other teams out of the corral, the pub's team, minus Brendan, entered the arena ever so cautiously. Instead of approaching the bull, they stood by the fence separating the bull and the cows. The bull kept alternating his attention between the intruders and the cows behind them. He must have been concentrating very hard on whether the new additions to the corral were a threat, or perhaps he was just wishing they would get out of his way so he could gander on the cows and make his selection. Regardless, he was not paying attention behind him. Brendan walked up behind him very stealthily and with a quick motion jumped on the bull's back. The bull bucked and twirled around several times while Brendan hung on to its neck. Brendan eventually put himself into a position so he could bend down and placed his lips next to the bull's ear. The bull seemed to stiffen and shook his head up and down, he then moved his head left and right. He then fell to the ground rolled over on his back and laid there waiting for the ten count. Brendan gave a signal to the members of the team and they all came forward and sat on the bull's stomach, counted to ten and immediately hopped off and retreated to the fence while the bull regained his footing. The bull then walked over to the adjoining corral, being escorted by Brendan, who opened the gate and let the bull in to "visit" the other detainees so to speak. The team from O'Brian's Black and Tan won the field.

During our celebration at the pub that evening I got Brendan aside and asked him what exactly happened and asked how he pulled off such a feat.

"Well you see, sir, I come from a long line of bull whisperers. You not being from these parts I suspect, know that whenever we transport a bull from one breeding function to another we have to do it by cart. Some bulls can get very obstinate and cause a lot of havoc, so a bull whisperer is hired to sit in the back of the cart, and place a bull restrainer on its testicles so the bull does not have a desire to move about in the cart. We whisper to the bull during the entire trip and he gets to recognize our voice and equates our voice with what is probably a great discomfort to the bull. If the bull protests a lot, the restraints are tightened. All I did once on the bull's back was to whisper in the bull's ear if he remembered me. You noticed that he shook his head up and down. I asked him if he wanted me to put the restraints on him again and he shook his head from side to side, meaning no. I then told him that if he would lay on his back and let me and my team mates sit on his stomach for a bit I would let him get up, walk him over to the cows and let him into the adjoining corral. Bulls are not stupid creatures, you know."

The butcher and I decided that we would let nature take its course and given a couple of days, since he is rather an old bull, he would wear himself out and die of natural causes, avoiding the knife.

Chapter 10
The Emerald Buffalo

I have seen several people who are internationally famous. I have shaken hands with a couple of senators, one president, and even a man who shook the hand of Neil Armstrong, but I cannot truthfully say I have "met" them, let alone, call them friends. However, there are many who reach the pinnacle of their profession and are icons to a small but fanatical following. I do know one of those types and even count him as a friend.

Bev and Abdul were contemplating how the menu at the pub could be improved. We had plenty of Irish dishes, pastas, Mexican food, and schnitzels, but just lacked what one might call the signature dish. While they were stewing over the matter, I was reading the latest addition of *Pub Weekly International.* As I turned the page I saw that Dublin was holding its annual barbeque competition and that the featured judge was none other than the world-renowned barbeque chef extraordinaire Bill Pittman. The advertisement went on to say that he would hold a special demonstration of the finer points of barbequing, using his famous mobile barbeque pit known the world over as The Emerald

Buffalo.

Bill started his barbequing career on a regular charcoal grill. Being a fireman, he had plenty of time on his hands between fires and rescuing treed cats to hone his ability. He modified a discarded grill he had found at the site of a house fire. He became so proficient in his preparation and cooking technique, and the charcoal apparatus he improved on became so ingenious, that he was soon doing all the cooking for the firemen at his station. Word spread around the other station houses and they clamored for his food. At about the same time, the labor contract ran out with the city and an agreement was finally reached only after Bill was given one duty-free day each week to prepare barbeque for the entire department.

He continued cooking for the department in this fashion until he retired, and then he started entering local competitions, winning most of them. He kept entering bigger and bigger contests and eventually won the New York City Barbeque Open, the Memphis Regional, the Atlanta Southern Invitational, and the Kansas City Royal Barbeque Masters. He got an agent, acquired some sponsors, made several endorsements, and began entering international events that were held in Europe and Australia. His crowning achievement was winning the prestigious Paris International Cuisine of Barbequing event. Bill was thus established as an icon to those who follow barbequing, and to this day is treated like a rock star wherever he goes, demonstrating techniques and judging those who dream of achieving the same success.

I had not seen Bill for many years and suspected he had no idea I was in Ireland or even if I was still alive or if he had thought about me much if at all. I thought it would be great sport to show up at the Dublin event and surprise him. One thing might be a problem, I thought, and that was how I was going to get around the security that must follow him wherever he went. But that was a problem I would face when I got there. I let it be known in the pub that evening that the next day I would head for Dublin.

As I suspected, the arena Bill was to perform in was packed and security guards were surrounding the place. I went up to one security guard and told him I was a friend of Bill's from the States and wanted to say hello.

"Yeah, you and everyone else, move along mate." That was about as nice a response as I got from all the other guards I asked.

I was just about to chalk my trip to Dublin as a misadventure when I spotted a familiar face talking to one of the guards. From a distance it appeared like he was giving orders and directions so I suspected he might have some authority. As I approached him I kept trying to figure out who he was and if I really did know him. Just as I was about to tap the guy on the shoulder he turned around and cried, "Snapper? What in the world are you doing here? I can't believe this!" As soon as he spoke I realized who I was talking to. "Well my gosh Skip, this is a surprise. What are you doing here?"

Skip was Skip Coombs. He was a year behind me in school and the last I heard he had joined the Marines and gone to Viet Nam. I remembered that he and Bill had been good friends. We spent a few minutes catching up and explaining to each other why we found ourselves after 45 years or so standing in front of the Civic Arena in Dublin. Not to dwell on what he was doing there, but the short story is that after he retired as a financial manager he went to work for Bill as his road and business manager. I asked him if he thought it was possible for me to say hello to Bill. He would do better than that and escorted me to Bill's trailer where he was preparing for the night's demonstration.

Bill was surprised to see me, as you might expect, but we were not able to do a whole lot of catching up right then because Bill was on in a few minutes. It was decided that I would sit with Skip and watch the demonstration and afterward visit some more.

The presentation Bill gave was impressive and words cannot describe the skill and dexterity he displayed, so I will not try. Besides, Skip told me that licensing and copyright prevented any descriptive publication.

After Bill was through we all sat around and had a drink or two and discussed the old times and all the things old friends discuss after absences of almost five decades.

When we began to repeat stories I thought it was

time to leave and Bill asked me to stay the night. I thanked him but said I needed to get back, that I had a pub to run.

"That's too bad," he said. "Bobbie will be disappointed she missed you."

"Bobbie?" I asked.

"Yes, you remember Bobbie Martin don't you? She travels with me a lot and acts as my on-the-road spiritual adviser."

Well, of course I remembered Bobbie. She had gone to high school with us also and had known Bill and Skip ever since elementary school. I asked if he and Bobbie were an item now and he said no, that she was his spiritual adviser and kept him and Skip on a moral compass during their tours. He explained that "Paul and Ringo told me that such guidance was necessary when one toured internationally." (I guess international icons have their own little network.) "She won't be back till tomorrow morning, however, because she's writing a book on spirituality and doing some research at an all-night Druid ceremony."

I was disappointed but I really did have to leave. I told him to give her my best and if they had some down time to swing by Devere and stop in for a pint and a new sandwich I had just thought of.

"I think I will call it the Bill Pittman."

Bill looked a little distressed and said that he could not authorize the use of his name. "You cannot believe international copyright and licensing laws. We would both get into trouble. I do have a suggestion, though."

I stayed a little longer, we all hugged in a manly fashion and I started my journey back to Devere.

Bev and Abdul at last have a signature dish for the menu and the new item has proven to be a big hit at O'Brian's Black and Tan. It is a barbeque pulled beef or pork sandwich called the Emerald Buffalo. Coleslaw and baked beans are extra.

Chapter 11
A Little Vote

Two years ago an astounding thing happened in Devere: a Leprechaun was elected to the village council. This had never happened before. The Leprechaun community is not large, nor were they active in local politics before that, and they never seemed to agree on anything amongst themselves anyway. The Catholic and Protestant majority would always court the "Little Vote," as it was referred to, and now and then throw a shamrock their way, but all in all the Little Vote was not considered important, let alone threatening to the status quo.

From out of the green, however, a leader arose from the Leprechaun community that was able to pull all the different Little factions together. He was a little taller, a little less green, and more educated than most Leprechauns. His rhetoric was superb. His ability to speak about how things should be, and the wholesomeness and kindness he projected, appealed to the historically ignored, and also to more than a few Catholics and Protestants, who were normally at odds with each other anyway.

It was the first time a Leprechaun had run for office as a serious candidate and the Leprechauns, along with the Dwarf community, voted in a block. That, along with the disenfranchised Catholics and Protestants, ensured John Littleman was elected councilperson of District Two. District Two just so happens to be the district the pub was in, and the pub had the added distinction of being the polling place for the village. It is a great honor and I respect the fact that the sale of alcohol is not allowed until one has cast his or her vote.

After John Littleman took office, it seems like he could do nothing right—at least that's what the Catholics and Protestants that had not defected to John's side contended. They had a point, because every time he would introduce a village ordinance, it would either be shelved or voted down. The promises he had made, he was unable to fulfill, and he took much abuse from those who were against his policies. Most of those who were opposed to what he espoused did so because they considered his positions radical, but those who opposed him most did so because he was a Leprechaun. They let those who opposed John Littleman based on his governmental philosophy take the lead in the vocal opposition, while the anti-Leprechaun forces egged the others on and financed the hate campaign, hidden from critical analysis.

John Littleman was a gentleman, though, and took the attacks and hidden slander in stride and just chalked it all up to politics. Because of his success in at least getting elected, some other Leprechauns and one Dwarf decided to run for the council seats coming up for election this November.

The village leaders, elected and unelected, realized that if the Leprechauns, Dwarfs, and disgruntled Protestants and Catholics voted as a group again, the village "will be run by a bunch of midgets."

To counter this threat, the village council passed an ordinance that stated that milk crates would no longer be provided by the village election commission for those who happened to be too short to reach the polling booth. The ordinance went on to say, however, that any voter could bring their own device that would boost them vertically—but only after a safety inspection certificate was provided to the election commission certifying that the device was not a hazard.

A protest was immediately made by John Littleman to the village council. He demanded to know why, after all these years, such an ordinance was necessary. In unison the other members of the council said nothing.

I don't know if not having milk crates provided by the village on election day will hinder the Leprechaun and Dwarf turnout or not. They are allowed to bring their own, the ordinance says, and the people who support the measure insist it is because of the liability issue, and besides, "What's the big deal anyway, if they're too lazy to get their own milk crate, they shouldn't vote."

In our weekly pub business meeting the matter

was discussed and we thought that perhaps we could rent milk crates at the font door when people came into vote. Then when they finished voting they could redeem the milk crate at the bar and get a "free" drink. Bev suggested that if people turned in a milk crate that we had not rented, we would charge half of what we normally would, and thus create a surplus of milk crates for the next election to be rented at a reduced price. How does she come up with these ideas? Anyway I have not played politics for a long time, and did so now only reluctantly, but the combination of doing one's civic duty and making a dollar or two is irresistible.

Chapter 12
Lake Donnie Mann

Lake Donnie Mann is the largest lake in the County of O'Malley. As one might expect, it was named after a chap called Donnie Mann some years ago but until just recently that was all I knew, partly because I never bothered to ask.

A man will lie to his wife. He will lie to his priest. He will lie to the Garda. In fact, a man will lie to just about anyone or anything if he thinks the truth will cause him pain or embarrassment or increase or decrease his status in the community. One person, though, he will never lie to is his pub keeper—at least, no more than I would embellish any of my tales.

It was late. The pub was about to close. The last patron was Shamus O'Malley. Outside, the wind picked up and the shutters blew open. Shamus, a few cups into his own wind, helped me close and secure the window shutters. For his help I drew him one more pint and we began to chat. As he was about to finish his free brew I indicated it was time to leave, but felt a little bad about putting him out in the pounding wind and rain. He was feeling about the same, I guess, because he asked me if he could stick around a little longer. Well he looked so low I couldn't say no, so I drew another pint, which he paid for, and we continued our aimless conversation.

We eventually got around to talking about fishing, which finally led me to ask how Lake Donnie Mann got its name. I did not expect illumination, let alone a saga. He hunched over his beer, looked over his shoulder, and said, "Since you have shown me some kindness, I will relate to you a story told to me by my Grandfather. It is not a secret story, but no one believes it except me, and I have been made fun of more than once in my telling.

"Grandfather was an honest man. He swore to me that what I am about to relate is a true story and I believe him. I have no children, thus no grandchildren, so I might as well tell you, because if I did have children they would be about your age. After hearing it feel free to pass it on to whoever you want—just be prepared that knowing the truth does not always free one from ridicule. Not relating the story as often as I think it deserves has burnt a hole in my soul for many years. I have been afraid I would die without anyone believing me, and I sense you will.

"Donnie Mann was a trader in salt. He would pick up a load of salt at one end of the lake and deliver it to the villages dotted around the shore. It was the custom in those days for people to name their boat after themselves, and The Donnie Mann was known far and wide, and so dominated the salt trade and other necessary cargo delivery that people started referring to the lake as Donnie Mann's. Donnie Mann was a proud and arrogant man and began to think of the lake as his own and himself as its master. But it seems the lake had a mind of its own.

"It was sort of a night like tonight my Grandfather said. The wind was howling, the waves were gigantic, and it was blustering cold. Donnie Mann had one more load of salt to deliver and he sat here in this very pub with his three-man crew waiting for the storm to pass. But pass it did not. Donnie Mann became impatient. He decided to make the run across the lake to deliver his last load. He was bound and determined to leave and collect a large fee for his even larger stash of salt this trip. Everyone in the pub, even his crew, begged him not to go. He would not listen, and called his crew a bunch of cowards when they refused to accompany him. He marched down to the docks, set sail, and Donnie Mann and The Donnie Mann were never seen nor heard from again...or so it was in the lifetime of those in the pub that night. Eventually the lake began to be called Lake Donnie Mann."

Well, I thought that was interesting but it didn't seem much like a story others would disbelieve and ridicule, and I told him so.

"Me lad, that is only half the story." He continued: "Many, many years later a fishing boat came across a drifting derelict floating aimlessly far from shore. The crew realized that the derelict was crewless and must have been abandoned, so thoughts of salvage took the place of fishing.

"When they boarded they searched for cargo but found none. They did not understand why the boat had been abandoned, because it was in pretty good shape. Their search eventually led them to the helm, where they found the ship's log. They had a somewhat limited interest in books, but they did realize it might help to secure salvage rights. Instead of reading the log right away, they gave it to the youngest member of the crew for safekeeping. That was my Grandfather.

"They secured the boat for towing and headed toward land. It had been a clear day but from out of nowhere a northern squall appeared. It was like the lake had its own idea about salvage rights, and would not give up the boat it had claimed it as its own. Both boats were capsized and sunk with all hands lost, save my Grandfather, who was found two days later clinging to the side of an overturned dinghy.

"At the formal inquest at the Maritime Court held in Dublin, an investigation tried to determine what had actually happened to the fishing boat. They called my Grandfather to give testimony. They believed him about the storm, the capsizing, and the loss of the crew. When asked if there was any indication as to the name of the boat trying to be salvaged is when doubt crept into the proceedings. 'Twas called 'The Donnie Mann', me Lord, Grandfather told the Court. From that statement he would not budge, although he was laughed at and threatened with imprisonment for piracy gone awry.

"More rational thought finally prevailed, given my Grandfather's youth, and the Court took pity and cleared him of any wrongdoing. They did order that since The Donnie Mann had gone missing over a hundred years ago, it could not have possibly been the boat in question. The poor lad must be delusional, the inquest determined, and he was ordered to the Saint Patrick's Hospital for the Insane until such time as Grandfather could sort fact from fiction. At that time, and no sooner, could he be released.

"Grandfather decided after three months of incarceration that unless he changed his story he really would become insane, and realized that honesty and integrity were not that important. He petitioned the court and changed his story, saying he realized he must have been hallucinating after all. Grandfather returned to Devere, took up farming, and never sailed on a ship again."

I immediately saw a flaw in his story, an inconsistency, one that did not close the loop to any great mystery. The story, I decided, was just a bunch of the blarney.

"What happened to the Ship's Log that was given to your Grandfather? I suspect he lost it when the ship went down, didn't he?" I was trying to give him an honorable way out of the corner he had told himself into.

"Well, yes, the Log was lost. Like I said, he was

floating around for two days clinging to a dinghy. Having been given the Log Book for safekeeping, he had tied it around his neck. While he was floating around he had nothing to do so he started reading the Log. Most of the log had been ruined and he only was able to read the cover page and the last entry with any clarity, and other bits and pieces. The cover had 'Ship's Log: The Donnie Mann.' Captain Donnie Mann's last entry was: 'Too much salt, ship taking on water, am foundering.' He had always heard about Donnie Mann and realized he held an answer to a mystery in his hand. He also realized that he would probably die alone at sea and his discovery concerning The Donnie Mann would never be known. He began to carve on the side of the dinghy a very short version of what I just told you.

"He eventually passed out, and when he awoke on a lifesaving trawler that happened by, his rescuers had no knowledge of the Log and the dinghy had not been retrieved. The Log, no doubt, was destroyed, and it and the dinghy rested somewhere at the bottom of Lake Donnie Mann. It is a story that is true. Grandfather had no reason to lie, but without proof he was never believed outside the family, and he spent the rest of his life walking along the lake shore early in the morning, just in case the dinghy had broken apart and a telltale portion drifted ashore. If one did, it may not have been actual proof of his story, but it seemed more important to him the older he became."

The wind and rain had calmed down. We made a little toast to Donnie Mann, The Donnie Mann, Lake Donnie Mann, and finally Grandfather, and bid each other a good night.

Over biscuits and coffee the next morning I was relaying the story to Bev. She looked nonplussed and said it was a mystery, but not a great mystery.

"I have heard something like that before, but off the coast of Nova Scotia. As I remember the story my Great Uncle Vinnie was smuggling a load of whiskey from Canada. He overloaded the boat and when a northern squall came up the weight of the whiskey in the casks was too much and the boat went down. Uncle Vinnie and the crew survived but the loss was not made known to the authorities, naturally. Some months later the boat reappeared about the same place where Uncle Vinnie claimed it had sunk. The Coast Guard traced the registration to a corporation in Chicago but the company did not exist, naturally, and those listed as company executives and board members were all dead, according to Cook County records. The Coast Guard was at a loss to explain anything. It was Uncle Michael who postulated among the family that the whiskey had probably seeped from cracks in the kegs while on the bottom, caused by the pounding storm, lightening the load and allowing the ship's normal buoyancy to bring it to the surface. If The Donnie Mann was overloaded with salt the weight could have easily taken it to the bottom, and when the salt eventually dissolved, the ship would resurface. If The Donnie Mann's cargo compartments were watertight, as one would expect it to be in the salt trade, dissolving could take a long time, and given the coolness of the lake bottom, the wood would have rotted more slowly than normal. What little wood rot that had taken place would not have prevented it floating again. The boat became lighter at the bottom of the lake, ergo up she went."

Well, I can always count on Bev to come up with a rational solution to any mysterious encounter I come across.

Ray the Raven and I went out for our morning walk along the banks of Lake Donnie Mann, as we did every morning, and as every morning we passed Shamus O'Malley doing the same. This time, though, we eyed each other knowingly, like we shared a secret, which in fact we did. I will never be able to walk the lake shore again without keeping a lookout for flat pieces of driftwood that just might have come from a dinghy supposedly lost many years ago.

Chapter 13
Darwin Cherries

While out on one of my weekend walk-a-bouts, I came across a grove of trees that after closer examination was an orchard. Not being one who knows one tree from another, I was not sure what type of orchard it was. It was very well-kept and I noticed that between the rows of trees there were potato hills.

I sat down to rest when I noticed an old man walking between the trees and mounds straight towards me. I figured he was the owner and was going to tell me I was trespassing and for me to leave. Quite the contrary. He introduced himself as Jamie O'Rilley and yes, he was the owner of the orchard, and the trees were cherry. He was a very nice sort of chap and talkative, too.

He told me he had been developing this cherry orchard for over 20 years and it produced more cherries per tree than any other like-sized orchard in the country, possibly the world. I told him that I really never associated Ireland with cherry trees and he said that is normally the case, but for some reason cherries seemed to flourish in these parts.

"Even the horticultural society in Belfast can't explain it," he said. "But here it is."

"Have you always grown cherries?" I asked.

"No, like most people in these parts I used to grow potatoes, but like most people it was boom or bust each season. I was reading a catalog one winter and decided to order a couple of cherry tree seedlings. Just for fun if for no other reason. I mean, how excited can one get over potatoes?

"When the seedlings arrived I followed the instructions very carefully and it seems like in no time at all I had some sprouts. The next thing you knew, I was able to plant some between potato rows. It was just a hobby at that point. I really never expected to see any cherries. However after a couple of years or so, there were some blossoms, and then the biggest, reddest, best-looking cherries I had ever seen appeared. I was just about ready to pick my first harvest when a flock of birds swooped down and ate every last one of the cherries right off the limbs.

"Well, I was a little annoyed, but it was not a great loss, for I had very little money tied up in the endeavor. I took it as a real challenge, however, and decided to outwit the birds. The next winter I got a bunch of rubber snakes and hung them from the branches. I had read that birds do not like snakes and thought that my decoys would scare them off. The next spring, there were blossoms, and cherries bigger and better than the year before, but the birds came again. I guess that since there are no snakes in

Ireland, the birds didn't know they should be afraid of them. I was not deterred.

"The next winter, I hung aluminum pie plates and strips from the branches. I thought that perhaps the glitter from the constant swaying in the sunlight would confuse the birds and even create an obstacle for them to land on the branches and eat my cherries. Well, as you can guess, that didn't work either.

"I decided that cherries were not in my future and I would just let the trees go to seed and fend for themselves. At least I would be feeding the birds through a natural process.

"It was around Christmas when I received a tin of popcorn from my cousin in America. It contained three different colored kinds of popcorn—yellow, caramel, and red. The yellow had a cheesy sharp cheddar taste much to my liking, the caramel as you would suspect tasted of caramel and satisfied my sweet tooth, the red would be cinnamon, I assumed. When I tried the red it was cinnamon, but it tasted terrible and burnt the inside of my mouth. I spit it out immediately. Who would eat this more than once, was my first thought. Then on my second thought it dawned on me.

"After the last snow of the winter, while the snow was a crystal white, I spread the hot cinnamon popcorn, doused by a little red pepper, on the ground under the cherry trees. The birds spotted the red specks on the ground and welcomed the early food supply. However, when they started eating the red popcorn it tasted to them like it did to me—even worse, I bet. They started identifying red with a hot bitter taste which they found repugnant and looked for another food supply, as it turned out.

"That spring, the blossoms came, the cherries came, and they have been coming ever since. The birds have returned but they are attracted to the insects that can ruin a potato crop, and the additional insects that are drawn to cherries, and not the cherries themselves. The birds don't leave this inexhaustible food supply of insects, thus increasing the fertilization required for my cherry trees and potato plants. Not only do I now have a huge cherry crop each year, I haven't had a bad year growing potatoes for a long time.

"Each year I add a few more trees, throw out some hot cinnamon popcorn laced with red pepper, and the result is what you see. I sell most of the product under the brand name of Darwin and have made a comfortable living."

"Darwin, Darwin Cherries," I said. "Uh, why not O'Rilley, Devere, or O'Malley cherries, after you or the community?"

"Oh, I don't know. The name just seemed to me like a natural selection."

Chapter 14
Fairy Tale

It was around closing time. O'Rilley, O'Malley, Doc Mike, McShane, and McDougan were finishing up and about to head home. Brian was taking inventory of the liquor and other odds and ends that had just come up, and Traci was talking to one bloke, looking at another and probably thinking of someone else. Bev was in the kitchen preparing cherry hummus and a couple of sack lunches, Abdul was busy sweeping and mopping the floor, and Ray the Raven was flittering around the pub snagging crumbs left by sloppy patrons. I was recovering from a busy night of socializing with the patrons and decisions that management needed to make due to a couple of unexpected events while sipping on a black and tan. All was normal, just a couple of things out of the ordinary, but then again, that was normal.

Just as I was thinking that my latest endeavor to help those less fortunate, meaning anyone other than my pub family, was a success, two men entered the pub. They were dressed in fedoras, trench coats belted at the waist, and very serious looking. I recognized what, but not who they were. Garda. Cops look the same all over the world. The best I can describe a Garda is that they are a cross between the RCMP, State Troopers, County Sheriffs, Scotland Yard, and the FBI.

They flashed their badges while introducing themselves as Detective Sergeant Tinker and Detective Inspector Darling. They said they wanted some information.

"We are looking for a couple of Fairies that are suspected of robbing the National Bank of Ireland in Hook County yesterday, and we have followed their trail to the door of your pub. Anything ring a bell?"

"We get a lot of people in here but I usually know most everyone," I said. "I don't recall specifically seeing anyone that would match what I'd think of as a Fairy's description recently. Feel free to look around," I said, realizing that I had technically not told any lies to the Garda.

For those of you who don't know about Fairies, let me back up and give you a little information. First of all, Fairies can change size and appear human, have green eyes and give off a slight radiance. They never age, or so it seems. They are even-tempered but when in a fight they like to bite. They treat nice people, places, and things nicely and bad people, places, and things badly. You never say thank-you to a Fairy, you just give them something that will guarantee remembrance.

Some say that they are a race that went into hiding

years ago and just now emerging into society and having a tough time coping with the complexities of non-Fairy civilization. I feel sorry for Fairies. They must have a hard life trying to fit into a society that one time felt like they needed to be chastised and ridiculed for being different.

For all their difficulties, a Fairy cannot lie. He may try to confuse you with words but he will never tell you a complete falsehood, nor the complete truth, if it is to his advantage to or not to do so. It is an art form that those of us who have practiced politics know well.

I am a law-abiding citizen and would never break the law unnecessarily, but I have always thought that law and justice might be two different animals. I do not condone stealing as such, and if someone is caught red-handed in any criminal act, they should be somewhat punished. From what the Garda told me, the National Bank of Ireland in Hook County was owned by a man named J. M. Barrie, a ruthless and cunning man, or so I have heard across the bar.

Gardas Tinker and Darling said the clock was ticking and they wanted to catch up with the culprits before they reached Never Landing, a swampy area just a few more leagues down the road. They said once the duo got to Never Landing they would melt into what is the largest Fairy community in Ireland and be almost impossible to apprehend, because "they are all the same you know," said one of Ireland's finest.

If anyone knew the seedier side of our community,

I told them, it would be my brother Brian. I called him from the back room and they asked him the same sort of questions I was asked. He gave the same information I had, which was little and none, but did it in such a slow and stuttering manner, I suspected they thought he was the village half-wit.

Brian and I felt under no obligation to give the Garda more information than they had requested. We believed all Fairies to be innocent in their own way. Mr. Barrie, we had been informed, had foreclosed on many a mother's farm while Fairy Volunteers had been fighting in the Banshee War several years ago and he, Mr. Barrie, was a very bad man and Fairies do bad things to bad people, and besides, no Fairy told me they had not robbed the bank and taken all they were accused of taking. The Fairies, I have been told, believed Mr. Barrie took the additional amount that was supposedly missing. The Fairies I might have known might have been in our pub just recently, and they might be making their escape out the backdoor while the Garda were talking to Brian with his sham stammering and stuttering. If that all is true, the two Fairies in question, Peter and Wendy, had a good chance of getting to Never Landing, if in fact such Fairies existed and were in the kitchen near the back door receiving a sack lunch from Bev an Abdul.

I offered the two Garda a drink on the house, but they declined and said they had to be on their way, that it looked like rain and the Fairy dust they were following would be washed away if they did not hurry.

As soon as they left our pub I told Abdul to wash down the back ally, because I suspected that it might be dusty. I told him he needed to concentrate his washing towards the North Star, which might just be the direction one would travel if one wanted to go to a little town just a few leagues down the road called Never Landing.

Chapter 15
Pickle Piercing

Abdul had learned a lot from Bev about food preparation and restaurant/pub logistics and he was very appreciative, so much so he has started teaching her the art of pickle piercing. She is making such good progress she is about to order her own pickle piercer. One cannot use another's pickle piercer once the training is over, they both tell me.

Devere recently has become known far and wide for its wonderful-tasting pickles. It is a phenomenon I am beginning to expect we owe to Abdul. Our pickles have a unique taste that has been written about in culinary magazines all over Ireland. I claim it is an old Irish recipe handed down generation after generation by family members, but that is really not the case. I have no real specific idea why our pickles taste the way they do, and recent enlightenment has made me decide I don't want to.

To get the best-tasting pickles, one has to retrieve them from the bottom of the barrel. This had always been done by dipping one's arm into a pickle vat up to the armpit and search the bottom until the pickle with just the right texture and firmness was found. Abdul thought this very unsanitary so he thought of a method to retrieve pickles from the bottom of the barrel by mechanical means.

During his days off Abdul would spend time with the cemetery caretaker, Peter Peck. Sometimes Peter would ask Abdul if he wanted to pick up some extra spending money by helping him probe old cemetery plots. Peter said that the church records had been sloppily kept in years past and sometimes when digging a new grave, they would come upon a vault, casket, or even a body buried without either, and would have to hurriedly find another place to dig, thus wasting a lot of time and effort. For some reason Abdul had a knack for and enjoyed grave probing and quickly learned to tell if a site was occupied or not by piercing the ground with the iron rod and feeling the thud of a vault, the cracking of a casket or the squishiness of pierced dead flesh.

Abdul, always being a resourceful sort, thought the same process might work retrieving pickles from the bottom of the barrel, and be much more sanitary. On his own he ordered his own grave probing device, an iron device three and half feet long and one eighth inch round, from the Interment Implement Company of Belfast. He made some modifications and in no time at all he could retrieve a pickle from the bottom of the barrel without said pickle ever touching a human hand, other than the person doing the ordering.

One afternoon Abdul received a phone call from the Parish Priest and was told to hurry to the cemetery. The Widow Twilly had just died. They needed to put her in the ground fast and Peter Peck was suffering from the gout. Abdul went to the pickle barrel, grabbed the pickle piercer and ran toward the door. I had a sickening feeling what was going to happen.

"Abdul, why don't you leave the pickle piercer here," I yelled. "We might need it."

"Not as much as the Widow Twilly might," he answered. "Besides, not to worry, boss. Every time I have used it in the past I clean it up real good."

Chapter 16
Potato Day

Brian and I were staying up late drinking our usual black and tan. Abdul had gone to bed much earlier due to some religious holiday he seems to come up with all the time. Bev and Ray the Raven were in the kitchen concocting some sort of special dessert for tomorrow's noonday crowd. How Ray the Raven was helping I am really not sure. Traci of course was still on her date and no telling when she would be home.

Brian and I were just about to give it up for the evening when Traci came home dragging one of the local home boys by the arm.

"Brian, Snapper, you got to hear this. Go get Bev, she ought to hear it also."

Bev came from the kitchen wiping her hands with a dishtowel with Ray the Raven resting upon her shoulder.

"Got to hear what?" I said.

"Tell'em Roy," Traci said.

"Well it isn't that big a deal," Roy the home boy began. "I just happened to ask what Devere's was planning to do this year for Potato Day."

All but Roy had puzzled expressions. Even Ray the Raven cocked his head to one side like he knew what was being talked about, and I am not sure half the time he doesn't know.

"O.K., young man," Brian said. "I'll bite. What are you talking about? Potato Day? I've never heard of it. What's that, some sort of day when we all dress up like potatoes and parade up and down the street?"

It was Roy's turn to look puzzled. "I thought you never heard of it. How did you know? Traci, you tell them."

"Oh, all right," Traci said, "I'll do the explaining. While you two over-protective big brothers hang around this pub of ours in the evening, I have been going down to the library studying up on local history. I came across an article in the newspaper archives about last year's Potato Day celebration. It sounded fun but I wondered if it was true or not. You know Snapper, you have always said that facts should not get in the way of a good story. Anyway, I went to the head librarian, which just so happens to be Roy here, and asked him about Potato Day. He confirmed the authenticity of the piece and was surprised no one had mentioned it to us already."

"That's about right, sir," said Roy. "All the businesses in the village sponsor an entry and if you don't, you might find yourself being shunned, even if you are the only drinking establishment in the village. It's the third most sacred holiday in Devere."

"Why is it so sacred?" Bev asked.

"According to tradition, there was a band of monks that could no longer stand the dictatorial way their Abbot conducted business in the monastery," Traci explained. "They were always being told what to do and how to do it, from the way they prayed to the way they ate. Life of a monk is hard, chaste, and full of poverty, but their religious leader was going beyond what they thought appropriate. Apparently the Irish Clan King that had established the order agreed with the Abbot and refused to acknowledge a new Abbot when a vote of the monks took place. Some of monks felt they had no choice but to leave and find a safe haven where they could practice their faith the way they felt was God's call.

"They walked for days, which turned into months, and just when they had run out of provisions, they were befriended by a group of Fairies. The Fairies took them in, and provided shelter and fed them over the winter. They taught the monks how to grow potatoes so they would become self sufficient in the future and even helped them build a monastery, which eventually became our church here in Devere.

"After the first year harvest of their first crop of potatoes, a celebration of thanks was in order. As the population grew, so did the celebration of thanks, and like most holidays started taking on modern characteristics until it became what it is.

"On or about the fourth Saturday after the third Sunday after the first full moon in November, the whole town gathers in the square. Each person dresses up like a potato and they march from the square to the church where a celebration of thanks is given. We have to figure out what we will wear this year." Traci concluded.

The story had a familiar ring and I tried to figure out why, but my pondering was soon overtaken by the practicalities of trying to figure out what kind of apparel could be made to look like a potato that wouldn't make us all look like Mr. Potato Head. However I was sure that Bev could figure out something. As Bev was tossing out different ideas about how we would dress and what kind of potato we would dress like, Traci said that Bev did not have to concern herself with what Traci would wear or what kind of potato she would be.

Traci and Roy looked at each other with a moonstruck puppy dog expression and Roy said, "Traci will be my sweet potato this year."

Brian and I looked at each and rolled our eyes. I guess Traci would be spending a lot more time at the library.

Chapter 17
Jackpot

Most of us have fantasized on what we would do if we were to win the Big One. I mean the one that would set up your family for generations to come. I mean the one that would provide your grandchildren's grandchildren with more money than they knew what to do with. I don't know what that amount would have to be, but I am sure that lottery officials could send you in a direction to find out. But such is my luck, the lottery numbers never seem to fall my way. Not directly, anyway.

The *National Enquirer* is not the type of newspaper you should probably base a lot of your knowledge about world affairs on, unless you have a desire to keep up with Elvis and UFO sightings or alien abductions of the third kind. I never read such trash and feel far superior to those who do, however, now and then a headline appears that is so sensational that one has to stop and ponder the possibilities. Abdul reads the *Enquirer* every week and when he's finished, throws it in the trash. I just sort of happened to notice it there every Saturday afternoon at three o'clock right behind the garbage container near the corner of our back ally in the white plastic container drawn tightly with a yellow bow. Pure coincidence, you see.

The headline read "Three Women Share in Power Ball." The sub-headline stated "All were married to the same man at different times in their lives." Well, that is certainly enough to get one's attention, if one has not much to do while dumpster-diving. The first line of the article gave me a little shortness of breath. "The ladies, which live in Kansas City, MO, Owaso, OK, and Tucson, AZ, are scheduled to meet with lottery officials in Des Moines, IA soon." Now what are the odds, I asked myself. They are the same towns Jan, (Dad's first wife) Doris (Dad's second wife,) and Marsha (Dad's third and last wife) live in. Nah, it cannot happen, the odds are too great.

I went back in the pub and poured myself a cup of tea. Brian came in and I casually asked him if he or Traci had spoken to their mom (Doris) lately? No, he said, and asked if I'd spoken to my mother (Jan).

"No, not for a week or so."

Traci walked in poured herself a cup of coffee. I asked if Traci had spoken to Marsha (stepmother to all) lately. "No," she replied.

I sort of chuckled to myself and quoted the article the best I could. They laughed along with me. Bev came out of the kitchen wondering what was so humorous. After relating the story I had read in the *Enquirer*, Bev saw the outlandishness of the possibilities. "Besides," Bev said, "Don't you think one of them would have called us by now?"

Just then Abdul came through the front door with

a Western Union Telegram. "I got this message yesterday. Sorry, I forgot to give it to you."

The telegram read: "Are arriving by three o'clock cart Tuesday [stop] Interesting news [stop] prepare three rooms [stop] Hope there is room at the inn [stop] Marsha." We had two days to get ready. For what, though, I was not certain.

*****

Inheriting a lot of money is an awesome responsibility. I was not taking it lightly. Of course I did not know for certain how much I would be receiving, but I expected it would be several million. I was bound and determined not to let the windfall change me or my way of life. A trip now and then, perhaps a new car, an Italian handmade suit, Gucci shoes, catered meals...you know, just the necessities of life.

Brian and Traci were not as fortunate as I, because they would have to share the portion Doris would leave them. They were not overly upset, of course, but their needs would have to be scaled back and could only be half of mine. My mother had another son by a former marriage but he was pretty well off and while I am not a pauper, my assets do not match his. He probably would not care if mom's cut of the three-way pie were just given to me. Marsha had a daughter, Rene', who would get Marsha's share. So everything was as it should be. It never occurred to us that perhaps our mothers and Marsha had plans of their own that may not have included indulging their children who really didn't need anything anyway.

All of us scampered around to bring the pub up to standards that our mothers (Marsha included in the term mother because she had been part of our lives for over 30 years) would approve. It wasn't so much Brian and I that cared but Traci and Bev did want to show the moms that their boys were being well taken care of, a woman-daughter-wife-mother thing, I guess. Anyway the place sparkled, all was where it should be, and nothing was out of place.

They arrived promptly at three, like they said they would. It was great to see them and they were just as glad to see us, and were really impressed with what we had done with pub. We chatted about this and that but nothing of any consequence (meaning inheritance) was brought up, but that was O.K. We really enjoyed ourselves and for short periods forgot about when the grand announcement would take place and what the particulars would be—well, almost. They were enchanted by Ray the Raven and thought Abdul was a nice guy after they found out he was not a Muslim but a Baptist, as proved by his wearing of an Irish Baptist Convention name tag.

After dinner that night Doris was the one who broached the subject.

Doris: "Well, you all might want to know the particulars that found us, the three of us, visiting all of you and partaking in such a lovely Italian meal. We three won the Lottery of sorts."

I guess I was the first one to pick up on the words "of sorts." What do you mean by 'of sorts, Doris?'

Marsha: "Let me answer that. I had gone to Oklahoma for a church convention and stopped by to see Doris. We chatted and decided that it had been years since we had seen the Grand Canyon and decided to drive out that direction. When we got to the Arizona state line I mentioned to Doris that the last time I had been in Arizona was when your Dad and I stopped in Tucson on our way to California and looked your mother up, Snapper. Doris, always the adventurer, said she had met Jan a couple of times and why don't they just change plans a little and drop down to Tucson and say hello. Who knows, Doris said, Jan may want to go to the Grand Canyon also."

Jan: "So they did. I must admit I was very shocked because I had not seen either one of them since that time at Mama's house when all three of us were there for one reason or another and Ted was helping Rene's boyfriend fix his car or something. I thought it very funny to see Ted so uncomfortable."

Doris: "I thought so also."

Marsha: "Me too, but I wasn't about to say anything because I had to go home with him that night."

"Well," I said, "I remember that also, but how did you win the lottery?"

Brian, Traci, Bev and I were finally told the story. Although all three women told different parts of the story at different times and sometimes and the same time, let me try to consolidate it for brevity's sake.

Doris, Marsha, or Jan: "We talked about what we all had been doing and who perhaps we had been doing it with, just girl talk. Then we talked about all the kids and grandkids and as you might suspect we talked about Ted. It was funny that we all had similar stories about our lives with him, but there was just enough difference in every one's age and his at the time we were together, that he was a different man when we each knew him. But there was a continuity that made things very similar when it came to his basic personality. Places and times change, but people don't, or at least not a whole lot.

"Now we are not here to talk about all that. That was then and this is now. For one reason or another we decided to buy a lottery ticket, you know, just for fun. We thought about just getting an automatic pick but decided to pick the dates of our children's birthdays. However we were two numbers short. So we picked Ted's birthday and the date we bought the ticket.

Well, we hit five out of six numbers. The date we bought the ticket was the one we missed. So instead of the multimillions we only won $50,000.00 apiece after taxes.

"We decided we would all take an around-the-world trip and thought what a better place to start than visiting the kids in Ireland. We will leave here tomorrow, for Dublin, then Belfast. Then on to London, Paris, Rome, Berlin, Istanbul, New Delhi, Hong Kong, Tokyo, Anchorage, and San Francisco.

Jan will go back to Arizona, Doris to Oklahoma, and Marsha to Kansas City. If we are real lucky, we will have spent all the money by the time we get home.

"I think it is about time to go to bed now. We leave tomorrow morning and have a busy schedule ahead of us as you can see."

Well as you can tell, my Gucci stuff was a thing of the past, but I really didn't care. It was nice to see them all together and happy.

I suspect Brian and Traci felt the way I did. For me it might have been a little deeper feeling, because I knew all three, whereas Brian and Traci had only known two. Here they were, three women off on the adventure of their lives, all of whom I knew at different times in my life, and theirs and Dad's, and in ways that may seem hard to explain, loved every one of them in different ways and still do. You love many different people in life for many different reasons, Mom always told me. Each had done something special for me. They may not remember some of the kindness they displayed when I needed it the most, but I do. I have a good memory and a long one.

That night Bev asked me if I thought it strange that Dad's ex-wives seemed to be friends 'of sorts' or at least comfortable and compatible with one another.

"No, not really," was my reply.

"What is it they have in common then?"

"They all married Dad," I said.

Epilogue
A New Chapter

Like when Bev and I went to Alaska the last time, instead of the two or three months we had planned to stay it ended being a year, the same happened in Devere. I think our mothers and Marsha's visit made us a little nostalgic and homesick. We began to miss the States.

Traci was the first one to broach the subject. She said that her and Roy had decided to marry and move back to Oklahoma and open up a western style steak house. She said that Brian and I could either buy her out or just send her share of the profits each quarter, whatever way we wished to handle it.

It was not long after that when Brian received a telegram from an old girlfriend who wanted to come visit him in Devere. She showed up one afternoon and two weeks later Brian informed Bev and me that he, too, was moving back to Oklahoma and made me the same offer Traci had made. That left Bev and me.

After Brian and his bride-to-be left, Bev and I reorganized things a little in the management of the pub. We promoted Abdul to chief bartender since he did not drink, hired Mic and Mac as Bev's two sous-chefs, and I took on more responsibility in planning and administering the pub's business affairs.

We talked about returning to the States also, and take up where we left off, spending half our time Tucson at the Far Horizon Village Resort and splitting up the other half of the year in Independence, Boston, and Long Beach, where our children and grandchildren were.

Up to this point, however, as I sit here writing about out latest adventure, we have come to no solid conclusion as to what we will do, when we will do it, or if in fact we ever will.

In the meantime, dear friend and reader, if you happen to find yourself in Ireland, in the County of O'Malley, in Devere along the shore of Lake Donnie Mann, stop in at O'Brian's Black and Tan. The first drink is on the house.

About the Author

Photo by Brian McAnally

Conley Stone "Snapper" McAnally is a retired U.S. Army Reserve officer and public school teacher. He is a former columnist for *The Examiner* of Independence, Missouri, where he cataloged his experience as a teacher in "bush" Alaska among the Yupik and Inupaque Eskimos. Several of his observations have been published in *Whispering Wind,* a magazine about Native American life and culture. His blog, The Adventures of Conley McAnally, is at conleymcanally.blogspot.com. He is also the the author of several short stories and novellas. He is the father of five children and grandfather of 15. He currently resides with his wife Beverly in Tucson, Arizona.

Pharaoh Publishing USA is an artisanal micropublisher of books, music and games in the Heart of America.

We do not accept unsolicited materials.

Contact us at pharaohpublishingusa@gmail.com.

14551792R00066

Made in the USA
Middletown, DE
19 November 2018